To my mom for always being there for me. I love you!
—Julia Cook

To my little girls, Sophia and Abigail.
—Carrie Hartman

Duplication and Copyright

Summary: Teaching children the concepts of personal space.

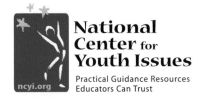

P.O. Box 22185
Chattanooga, TN 37422-2185
423.899.5714 • 800.477.8277
fax: 423.899.4547
www.ncyi.org
ISBN: 978-1-931636-87-2

Written by: Julia Cook
Illustrations by: Carrie Hartman
Published by National Center for Youth Issues
Softcover

Printed at RR Donnelley, Inc
Reynosa, Mexico
September, 2010

My name is Louis. People say that I have
a problem with personal space. I don't think I do. I am a space expert!!!!

Zoom! Zoom!

Zip! Zip!

Rip! Rip

Through the clouds...

Buzz the planets

Tickle the Sun

4

Back to Earth...

Now that was fun!

A few days ago, I wanted to show Betty Jean how gravity worked, so I jumped off a chair and did a "lunar landing" on the quiet rug. While I was in the air, Richard got in my way. I "lunar landed" on Richard's leg.

6

My teacher used her Cranky voice:

"Louis!" she said. "You are having problems with your personal space!"

"Why would she say that to me?" I thought. "I am a space expert!!!!!"

The other day on the playground, I was showing Rusty how comets sometimes smash right into satellites.

I was the comet.

Rusty was the satellite. When we smashed, the playground teacher used her cranky voice.

"Louis!" she said. "You have a problem with your personal space!"
Why would she say that to me? I thought. I am a space expert!!!!!

Abram had no idea what an eclipse was, so I showed him.

While he was talking to our teacher about his spelling test, I slowly walked right in between them and waved my hands in front of their faces.

My teacher used her REALLY cranky voice!

10

"Louis!!! You have a **BIG** problem with your personal space. I have just had it with you!!! Tomorrow, I am sending you to Personal Space Camp in Principal Goodkid's office."

Wow! I thought...Now I'll really be a space expert!!! I was so excited!! I didn't know that Principal Goodkid was a space expert, too.

11

So I ran home and told my mom about
my special invitation.
"It's about time!" my mom said.

The next day was my Very important day! I couldn't wait to get to school. I thought about all of the cool things that I was going to get to do at Personal Space Camp. I wondered if our lunch would be served in vacuum-packed space food bags like the real astronauts get.

"Maybe we'll even get to eat space ice cream!"

I walked into the principal's office and there, spread out on the floor, were five large hula hoops. "We must be going to learn about Saturn's rings," I thought. "Please choose a hoop and sit inside of it," said my principal. "I knew it!" I said to myself. We're starting with Saturn."

"You are all here today because you are having problems with personal space," said Principal Goodkid.

"That's it!…I'm in here to be a teacher's helper."

15

"Does anyone want to tell me what personal space is?,
I raised my hand right away.
"Yes Louis," said my principal.
"I am a space expert!" I said.
"I can tell you everything you need to know about space. I have my own spaceship. It goes like this..."

Zoom! Zoom! Zip! Zip!
through the clouds Rip! Rip!

Buzz the planets

Tickle the Sun

Back to Earth...

Now that was fun!

17

"That's great, Louis," said my principal. "But I'm not talking about outer space. I'm talking about personal space."

"Personal space, outer space…What's the difference?" I asked.

"Well, Louis, let's pretend that the hoop you are sitting in is your own personal spaceship. Are you a good pilot?"

"The best there is!" I said. "I never crash!"

"What happens if I put four other kids inside your spaceship with you like this?"

"Now can you still be a good pilot?"

"No," I said. "I'm too squished."

"I can't even move!"

"That's because there are too many people in your personal space. Do you like the way that feels?"

"No!"

"**Other people don't like it either**!" said the principal, using her cranky voice.

Principal Goodkid told everyone to go back to their own hoop, which was a good thing because Rusty had forgotten to brush his teeth before school.

Principal Goodkid told us that personal space is the amount of space that you need to feel comfortable.

"Everybody has a **comfort bubble**," she said. "Your **comfort bubble** is usually about the size of the hoop you are sitting in. If you get out of your hoop and get too close to another person, you break their comfort bubble."

"That's when teachers use their Cranky voice," I said.

My principal took out a bottle of bubbles. She blew through the wand.

"Look at all of the bubbles," she said. "Are they all the same size?"

"No," we all agreed.

"Your comfort bubble will not always be the same size either," she said. "Sometimes it will be big, like when you are around a stranger," or in a new situation…

Other times it will be smaller, like when you are **around your family and close friends.**"

"Most of the time when you are at school, your comfort bubble needs to be the size of your hula hoop."

I started to realize that we were not going to talk about Saturn, or its rings.

21

Next, Principal Goodkid pulled out a big long rope with lots of knots in it.

Finally, I thought to myself, real space camp stuff!

"Does anyone know what this is?" asked Principal Goodkid.

"That's a gravity extension line," I said with pride. "It secures you to your spaceship so you don't float away."

"Not exactly," she said.

"This is a Personal Space Line-Up Rope (PSLUR for short)."

"Everyone grab a knot with their right hand. This is how far apart you should be when you walk with your class

in a line. If you put your arm straight out ahead of you, your fingertips will barely be able to touch the shoulders of the person in front of you. Everyone has plenty of room, and your comfort bubbles will not get broken."

We went out into the hallway to practice walking with the Personal Space Line-Up Rope, PSLUR for short.

I went to grab the red knot, and Rusty pushed me right out of the way. He wanted the red knot.

"Hey!" I said to him…"You just broke my comfort bubble! Please stay in your own personal space."

Principal Goodkid was proud of me because I didn't push Rusty back. Then she gave Rusty her cranky look.

I started to realize that we were not going to talk about a gravity extension rope, or what it does.

Winnie
the Beagle

25

When we got back to Principal Goodkid's office, she made us lie down on big white paper. She said we could pose any way we wanted to, and then she traced each one of us. Finally, I thought, we're getting to some real space stuff.

We got to cut out our own shapes, and then she asked us, "Why is having a shape of you useful?"

"You are helping us make a pattern for our spacesuits!" I said proudly.

"Not exactly," she said. "Your body cutouts show you just how much personal space you take up. When all of us are together in a group, we have to share space. The rug we are sitting on is shared space. If you stand up on your feet like this, you take less shared space than if you sit down on your pockets like this."

"Now everyone put their shapes down flat on the rug, said Principal Goodkid. "Look how much shared space they take up. Everybody's comfort bubble is breaking! This is what happens when you lie down on the rug in your classroom during story time."

"That's when teachers use their *cranky* voice," I said.

I started to realize that we weren't going to talk about making our own spacesuits, or what spacesuits do.

Suddenly, a light bulb went on in my head. Personal space wasn't what I thought it was at all!
"So that's why my teachers used their cranky voices," I thought to myself.

At the end of the day, Principal Goodkid gave all of us graduation certificates for Personal Space Camp.

When I got home, I told my mom all about my day.

Then I showed her my certificate.

My mom was very proud!

She stuck my certificate up on the fridge using the Very Important Stuff magnet.

The next day at school, my teacher let me share all that I had learned at Personal Space Camp with my class. I had now become a DOUBLE SPACE EXPERT!

Ever since I became a Personal Space Expert, my teacher hasn't needed to use her cranky voice with me. Well, except for yesterday, when my paper space shuttle did a "fly-by" right next to her ear..........

Zoom! Zoom!
Through the clouds...
Rip! Rip!
Buzz the Planets
Tickle the Sun

ZIP! ZIP.

Back to Earth...
Now that
was f.